For my yeh-yeh, Chuck Yee, who grumbled a lot!
—KM

To Ye Ye and Lao Ye, thank you for teaching me chess,
buying me candies and trinkets behind Mom's back,
cooking the most delicious meals, and giving me the
best childhood anyone could ask for.
—XY

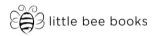 little bee books

251 Park Avenue South, New York, NY 10010
Text copyright © 2020 by Katrina Moore • Illustrations copyright © 2020 by Xindi Yan
Library of Congress Cataloging-in-Publication Data
Names: Moore, Katrina, author. | Yan, Xindi, illustrator. | Title: Grandpa grumps / by Katrina Moore;
illustrated by Xindi Yan. | Description: First edition. | New York, NY: Little Bee, [2020] | Summary: When Daisy's
grandfather, or Yeh-Yeh, visits from China, she does everything she can think of to make him smile and finally
finds a way. | Includes glossary of Chinese words and recipe for fried rice. | Identifiers: LCCN 2019018002 |
Subjects: | CYAC: Grandfathers—Fiction. | Chinese Americans—Fiction. | Mood (Psychology)—Fiction. |
Cooking, Chinese—Fiction. | Classification: LCC PZ7.1.M6556 Gr 2020 | DDC [E]—dc23
LC record available at https://lccn.loc.gov/2019018002
For more information about special discounts on bulk purchases,
please contact Little Bee Books at sales@littlebeebooks.com.
Manufactured in China   TPL 0320
First Edition   10 9 8 7 6 5 4 3 2 1
ISBN 978-1-4998-0886-5

littlebeebooks.com

GRANdPA GRUMPS

by
Katrina moore

illustrated by
Xindi Yan

little bee books

On Sunday, Daisy double-checked her list. "This will be the best week ever!" Yeh-Yeh was coming to visit from China. She couldn't wait to meet him!

Things to do with Yeh-yeh:
- Tea Party
- Build a Snowman
- Hot Coco (extra marshmellows)
- Kara-Oke
- Read Stories
- Draw!

"He's here, he's here!"

She looked at him closely.
She saw a head like her
daddy's, but with less hair.
A button nose, just like hers.
And a jolly, round belly,
perfect for hugging.

"Humph," Yeh-Yeh grumbled.
Hmmm, thought Daisy.
Grandpa isn't jolly.
Does he not like hugs?
She tried something else.
"Would you like some tea?"
Yeh-Yeh nodded.

"Hooray! Tea party!"
"Harrumph," Yeh-Yeh grumbled.
Grandpa's grumpy, thought Daisy. *This will not do.*
I have to make him smile before he leaves!

On Monday, Daisy popped
into Yeh-Yeh's room.
"I made hot cocoa—
with extra marshmallows!"
"Gah!" Yeh-Yeh grumbled.

On Tuesday, Daisy wanted
Yeh-Yeh to read to her.
Yeh-Yeh looked at her book.
He looked at Daisy.
"Hmmm," Yeh-Yeh grumbled.

He handed Daisy his newspaper instead.
"**Dú**," said Yeh-Yeh.
Daisy looked at his newspaper. She looked at Yeh-Yeh.
"**Do** . . .

. . . some art?"
Daisy hoped he'd smile—
but he didn't.

Day and night, Daisy tried to make Yeh-Yeh smile, and day and night—he didn't.

By Friday, Yeh-Yeh still hadn't smiled. This week wasn't turning out like Daisy hoped.

"Mama, why is Yeh-Yeh such a grump?"
"He shows love in other ways," said Mama.
Hmmm, thought Daisy. *How could I show Yeh-Yeh love in another way?*

Daisy had an idea!

She looked at her drawing.
She hoped he'd like it.

Daisy peeked into Yeh-Yeh's room.
No grumbling, no Yeh-Yeh . . . she was all alone.
She left his surprise on the bed,
and meant to leave—but she didn't.
What was this? Yeh-Yeh's newspaper . . . He saved it!

And what was this? A present!
He shows love in other ways, thought Daisy.

菜谱
RECIPE

Daisy had a new idea!

炒饭

2 茶匙植物油	1/3 杯青豆 1 茶匙姜末
1/2 杯洋葱切丁	2 杯熟米饭 盐和白胡椒适量
1/3 杯胡萝卜切丁	熟猪肉切丁 2 个鸡蛋
1/3 杯熟玉米粒	2 茶匙酱油

（请在成人监督下完成菜谱。请儿童远离明火。）

1. 将油倒入烧热的锅中，摇晃热锅。油要发出咝咝声。
2. 倒入洋葱，用中火炒到透明，再倒入胡萝卜、玉米、青豆、米饭和猪肉一起翻炒。
3. 倒入酱油并加入生姜、白胡椒和盐，翻炒均匀。
4. 在炒饭中间空出一个洞，漏出锅底。
5. 在洞中打入两个鸡蛋，开始炒鸡蛋。
6. 鸡蛋炒好后，将所有食材再次翻炒，直到鸡蛋也均匀炒入。
7. 享受美味吧！

On Saturday, Daisy waited for Yeh-Yeh.
"**Dú**?" asked Daisy.
Yeh-Yeh looked at the recipe card.
He looked at Daisy. He did not grumble.
"**Do** . . . to-geth-er," said Yeh-Yeh.
Daisy smiled and nodded.

"Rice?"

"R-ice," Yeh-Yeh said with a nod. "Fàn."

"Fà-n," Daisy repeated.

Yeh-Yeh pulled an egg from
the refrigerator and said, "Dàn."

"Dà-n," Daisy repeated.

Sizzle. Toss. Splash. Yeh-Yeh's hands danced.

"Looks funny," said Daisy.
"Hmmm," Yeh-Yeh grumbled.

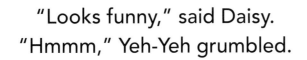

She tasted something sweet, but not like a marshmallow,
as well as something salty that sizzled and melted, just like a snowflake.
So many flavors—new, warm, exciting—were dancing around in her mouth!

"Chǎo Fàn," said Yeh-Yeh.
"Yum!" said Daisy. Her fingers wobbled.
She picked up a lump and dropped it . . .
right onto Yeh-Yeh's slipper.
He scrunched up his button nose.
"Oops!" She waited for Yeh-Yeh to grumble.

But he didn't.

Soon, Yeh-Yeh was laughing so hard,
his belly jiggled up and down.

Daisy thought he might pat her head—but
he didn't. Instead, he opened his arms wide.
It was the jolliest, most perfect, hug.

On Sunday, it was Yeh-Yeh's turn to surprise Daisy.
He hoped she'd smile. . . .

And she did.
It was time to make a new list!

Things to do with Yeh-Yeh in China:

- Fly a kite
- Ink Painting
- Sing a Chinese Song
- Eat Nian Gao (sticky rice cake)

1. Make Jiao Zi (Dumplings)

Yeh-Yeh's Chão Fàn

2 tsp. vegetable oil
1/2 cup finely diced onion
1/3 cup diced carrots
1/3 cup cooked corn
1/3 cup peas
2 cups cooked rice

cooked pork (diced into small cubes)
2 tsp. soy sauce
1 tsp. ginger
white pepper to taste
salt to taste
2 eggs

(This recipe should be made with adult supervision. Children should stay away from a hot stove!)

1. Pour the oil into a hot wok or pan and tilt the pan to spread the oil around until the entire surface is covered. The oil should sizzle.
2. Next, place the onions in the wok and cook them on medium heat until they are clear. Then, toss in the carrots, corn, peas, rice, and pork. Mix everything together.
3. Splash in soy sauce and add the ginger, white pepper, and salt. Give it all a quick toss.
4. Finally, when everything is sizzling and steaming, form a hole in the middle of the mixture so that the bottom of the pan is showing.
5. Break open 2 eggs and pour them into the hole. The eggs should begin cooking immediately.
6. After the eggs start to cook, stir all the ingredients together until the eggs are fully cooked and mixed in.
7. Enjoy!